A CHRISTMAS LESSON

Tom Krause Nicholas Child

Dedicated to all the wonderful children around the world

at Christmas time.

T.K

A cold winter's night in old London town, on a busy street corner, people bustling around, stood a father with his son collecting coins for the poor when the boy asked a question he had never asked before.

KRAUSE LANE

"Is there a purpose? Why are we here?"

the little boy asked as the yuletide drew near.

I really do hope that someday I will know

the reason we stand out here in the snow

ringing this bell as people walk by

while thousands of snowflakes descend from the sky.

The young boy exclaimed, "Father, where does it go, all the pennies we collect every year in the snow?

Why do we do it? Why do we care?

We work for these pennies, so why should we share?"

The father just smiled at his shivering son

who would rather be playing and having some fun

but soon would discover when the evening was done

the meaning of Christmas, the very first one.

"Because once a small baby, so meek and so mild,
was born in a manger, so humble the child."

"The Son of a King was born in this way
to give us a message he carried that day."

"You mean baby, Jesus?" Is He why we're here ringing this bell at Christmas time every year?"

"Yes," said the father, "That is why you should know about the very first Christmas a long time ago."

"The present God gave the world on that night

was the gift of his Son to make everything right."

"Why did he do it? Why did he care?

To teach about loving and how we should share."

"The meaning of Christmas, you see, my dear son,

is not about presents or just having fun

but the gift of a father, his own precious son,

so the world would be saved when his work was all done."

The words of the father touched the heart of his son.

He felt warm inside as a change had begun.

Sharing with others, not only just me.

Loving is giving. At last, he could see.

Now the little boy smiled - with a tear in his eye

as snowflakes kept falling from out of the sky.

He rang the bell louder as people walked by

while down deep in his heart, he finally knew why.

Merry Christmas to all from old London Town.

May your hearts be merry as you bustle around.

And never forget the lesson that was learned

by the boy, the gift of a Savior to give the

world joy.

Born 1957, Thomas Krause grew up next to the Missouri River in

Boonville, MO. in the USA. He went on to be a teacher in the Missouri

Public School System for thirty-one years.

He also became an author, poet, and National Motivation Speaker.

Contact Tom by email at: justmetrk@aol.com.

Nicholas Child is an illustrator based in the Cheshire countryisde in England. He has a love for illustrating people, animals and architecture so to work with Tom on this book was a wonderful experience.

www.thechildrensillustrator.com

CPSIA information can be obtained
at www.ICGtesting.com
Printed in the USA
JSHW070821280523
41978JS00019B/52